P9-DCQ-588

THE RESCUE MISSION

By **Maria S. Barbo**

Published by Scholastic Inc., *Publishers since 1920.* SCHOLASTIC and associated logos are trademarks and/or registered trademarks of Scholastic Inc.

ISBN 978-1-338-11290-0

12 11 10 9 8 7   17 18 19 20

Printed in the U.S.A.   40
First printing 2016

SCHOLASTIC INC.

"Look out, here I come!"
Bonnie shouted as she dove
into a big pile of leaves.

Dedenne and Pikachu
laughed.

They were all on their way
to the Pokémon Center in
Snowbelle City.

"Let's go, Bonnie," called her big brother, Clemont. He was a Pokémon Trainer. So were his friends, Ash and Serena.

Bonnie loved playing with their Pokémon. But she really wanted one of her own.

"So cute!" Bonnie shouted. A tiny green Pokémon had curled up inside her bag. It was sleeping. And it had the coolest pink mark on its tummy.

Bonnie knew she had to take care of it. She loved it already!

But when the little Pokémon saw her, it tried to hop away.

Bonnie grabbed it carefully. Then she showed it to her brother.

"Whoa!" said Clemont. "I've never seen that Pokémon before."

Ash checked his new Pokédex.

"Nothing," he said. "No data."

"So that means it's a new kind of Pokémon?" Clemont asked.

"Awesome!" cried Ash. "That's so cool!"

The little green Pokémon seemed scared.

"I'm going to take care of it," Bonnie decided.

"Bonnie!" Clemont warned. "You don't know anything about it."

But Bonnie knew she would learn.

"You're squishy," she told the Pokémon.
"So I'm going to call you—Squishy!"

"*Pika pika*," Pikachu warned, but it was too late.

The friends heard a loud rumble.

The ground shook.

"Oh no!" cried Ash. "Dodrio!"

A herd of Dodrio ran by and knocked everyone over. Their friend Sawyer was trying to catch one with his Grovyle.

Squishy got scared and bounced away.

"Hey," Bonnie cried, "my Squishy's gone!"

Squishy hopped as quickly as it could. But it did not get far.

Team Flare blocked its path. Their pack of angry Houndour growled.

"Trying to run away, are you now?" asked Team Flare's leader, Celosia. "We need you for Operation Z."

She called on her Drapion. "Pin Missile.
Let's go!"

A large purple Pokémon with giant claws
snatched Squishy.

Squishy squirmed, but it couldn't break
free.

"Good," said Celosia. "Let's go back to the
lab."

"You let Squishy go!" Bonnie shouted. She knew Squishy wanted their help.

"Please, what a bore," said Celosia. "Drapion, use Toxic."

Before Drapion could
make a move, Ash stepped
up.

"Okay, Pikachu," he said.
"Thunderbolt! GO!"

"*Pi-ka-chuuuuu!*"
Pikachu's cheeks sizzled
with a bolt of electricity.

"Grovyle," Sawyer shouted. "Use Leaf Storm!"

Grovyle blasted Squishy out of Drapion's claws.

Ash quickly called on Noibat. "Use Supersonic!"

Drapion tried to fight back with Sludge Bomb. But Pikachu zapped it with one last Thunderbolt.

The Houndour shrank back. Team Flare ran away. Squishy was safe!

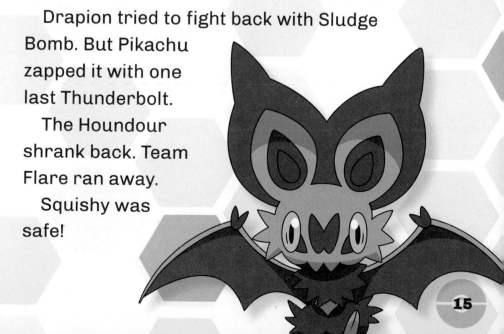

"Squishy, you're okay!" Bonnie scooped the Pokémon into a hug.

This time, Squishy did not try to hop away.

Ash, Clemont, Serena, and Sawyer threw their Poké Balls into the air. All their Pokémon came out to say hello.

"Squishy, these are your new friends!"
said Bonnie.

Squishy bounced up and down happily.

Soon all the Pokémon were sitting in a circle sharing food and water.

Pikachu held out some fruit. But Squishy would not eat it.

"*De ne*?" Dedenne tried to share a berry. Squishy shook its head.

Bonnie was worried. They'd had such a big day!

"Squishy, aren't you hungry?" she asked.

Squishy jumped up as if to say, "Don't worry. I don't need food."

It bounced over to a rock and curled up in a tiny patch of sunlight.

The pink mark on Squishy's tummy began to glow.

Squishy fell asleep smiling.

Bonnie's brother was confused, but Bonnie had an idea.

"Maybe all it needs is sunlight," she said.

"Wow!" said Serena.

Bonnie felt proud. They were learning about Squishy just by taking care of it.

The friends crawled into their tents and fell asleep. But Squishy woke up in the middle of the night with a bad feeling. Team Flare was back. Squishy knew it. This time, the Pokémon was not scared.

Squishy hopped into the forest. It would protect its new friends. And its new friends would protect Squishy.

"Squishy, wait up!" Bonnie cried. She ran after her Pokémon.

"*Pika pika!*" Pikachu called.

"I told you that Pokémon is mine, see?" Celosia held out a Poké Ball.

"Well, you're wrong," declared Ash. "If Squishy was yours, you wouldn't treat it the way you do!"

"Enough!" Celosia barked. "Dark Pulse!"

Her pack of Houndour shot sonic waves at Bonnie and her friends.

"Frogadier, Water Pulse," Ash shouted. "Pikachu, Thunderbolt!"

While Ash and Sawyer
fought, Clemont, Bonnie,
and Serena grabbed
their Pokémon and ran
for safety.
    Bonnie held Squishy
close.

But as they crossed a river, Bonnie
slipped on a rock.
Squishy fell into the water.
It was carried downstream far away
from Bonnie—right to Team Flare's Bisharp!

"We've got you now," said Celosia. "You're a Core Zygarde, and we need you for our experiment. So give it up."

Houndour and Sneasel snarled.

Squishy took a big hop backward.

Squishy wanted to find Bonnie and stay with her.

But it would need help.

If it really was a Core Pokémon like Team Flare said, then it must be the center of something big.

Squishy closed its eye and sent out a call. A mass of glowing Pokémon Cells came together around Squishy.

They spun and twirled until suddenly, Squishy took on a powerful new Forme!

Squishy's new Forme roared, and rays of light burst up from the ground.

"Retreat!" Team Flare screamed. They started running away.

From down the river, Bonnie heard the roar.

"It's Squishy, I know it!" she cried. She raced toward the sound.

"Squishy!" Bonnie ran to her Pokémon and hugged it tight.

"I won't let you go again," she said.

Squishy cuddled close. Bonnie had taken good care of the little green Pokémon, and it wasn't going anywhere without her.